Oh, I Am So Embarrassed!

SESAME STREET

CTW

A GROWING-UP BOOK™

By ANNA H. DICKSON
Illustrated by TOM COOKE

*Featuring Jim Henson's
Sesame Street Muppets*

On *Sesame Street*, Susan is performed by Loretta Long, Maria is
performed by Sonia Manzano, and Miles is performed by Miles Orman.

A SESAME STREET/GOLDEN PRESS BOOK
Published by Western Publishing Company, Inc., in conjunction with Children's Television Workshop.

One day Grover came home for lunch with Herry Monster.

"I'm glad you could come, Grover dear. I hope you like tomato soup and blueberry muffins," said Herry's mother.

"Oh, yes, thank you, Mrs. Monster," he said.

"Herry," she said, "you and Grover may go wash your paws, please."

The monsters ate lunch around the kitchen table.

"Grover, wouldn't you be more comfortable if you took off your baseball cap?" asked Herry's mommy.

"Oh, no, thank you," he said.

Just then Grover knocked over his glass of milk with his elbow. Milk spilled across the table, getting everyone's napkin wet.

"Oh!" said Grover. "I am so embarrassed."

"Don't worry about it, Grover," said Mrs. Monster. "It will wash right out." She mopped up the milk and poured him another glass.

Grover was so ashamed that he couldn't eat another muffin.

The next day Grover met his friends to play ball.

"Hey, Grover, cool baseball cap!" said Ernie. "May I see it?"

"Uh, no. I am sorry, Ernie." Grover looked down and counted his toes.

"Why not?" asked Ernie. "I'll be careful. I just want to try it on."

"I cannot take it off!" cried Grover.

Grover ran down Sesame Street and waited.

Whop! Herry kicked the ball so hard, it went flying.
Then it bounced and rolled down the sidewalk toward
Grover.

"I will get it. Let me get it. I have it!" yelled Grover,
and he ran to the ball. He reached out, but the ball
rolled right through his furry fingers and right
between his fuzzy feet and down the sidewalk.

Clang! The ball crashed into Oscar's can.
"What a catch, fumble-fingers!" said Oscar. "Remind me not to choose you for my team."
"Oh, I am so embarrassed," said Grover.

Just then a pesky little breeze sneaked up
Sesame Street and swept Grover's new baseball cap
off his head.

"OOPS!" said Grover. He put his hands over his face.
Everybody looked at him. Then everybody laughed.

"Grover, you have a new furcut!" cried Betty Lou.

"And it's really *short*," said Ernie.

"Yeah!" said Oscar. "Now, instead of a fur brain,
you're a fuzz head!"

Grover was so embarrassed.

"Don't feel bad, Grover," said Herry. "It will grow back. Your fur will be shaggy again before you know it!"

Herry handed Grover his hat. "Besides, I know something more embarrassing than going around in short fur," said Herry.

"What?" said Grover, pulling his hat firmly down over his eyes.

"Wearing water wings!"

"Water wings are for babies!" said Grover.

"But I can't swim yet," whispered Herry. "And that's not the worst part. My little sister doesn't have to wear water wings. She can already swim!"

"How embarrassing," said Bert.

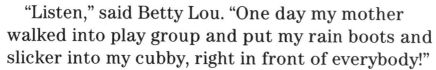

"Listen," said Betty Lou. "One day my mother walked into play group and put my rain boots and slicker into my cubby, right in front of everybody!"

"Oh, no!" cried Grover. He began to feel a little better.

"And then, after play group, I was the *only one* who had to walk home in rain boots and a slicker!" Betty Lou told them.

"Mothers can be so embarrassing!" said Telly.

"My daddy made me wear a *sweater* over my Halloween costume!" said Elmo.

"How could he?" gasped Grover. "I bet he said it was cold outside."

"Right!" said Elmo. "It was awful. I was this *scary* ghost. But when I put on my sweater to go trick-or-treating, nobody thought I was a real ghost! Everybody knew it was me!"

"Oh, that is terrible," said Grover.

"Guess what my mommy put in my lunch box instead of a peanut-butter-and-jelly sandwich one time," said Farley.

"What? What?" they all wanted to know.

"You are not going to believe this," said Farley. "A salad!"

They couldn't believe it.

"Eeew!" said Betty Lou.

"No cookies?" asked Cookie Monster.

"Weren't you embarrassed?" asked Telly.

"I was embarrassed once," said Telly. "My cousin
came to spend the night, and he found out my secret!
I was so embarrassed."

"What secret, Telly?" asked Elmo.

"That I like to sleep with the night-light on," he said.

Everybody laughed. Everybody else liked
night-lights, too.

"Well," said Elmo, "I still have to take naps! It's embarrassing."

"No!" said Oscar. "That's disgusting."

"Mommy says I get cranky before dinner if I don't have a little quiet time," said Elmo.

"That's OK, Elmo," said Big Bird. "Even grown-ups take naps sometimes."

"I did the most embarrassing thing of all," said Bert.

"Tell us, Bert," said Ernie. "We won't laugh!"

"Well, one day I went to the store wearing one saddle shoe and one *sneaker*. Oh, I was so embarrassed."

"Hee-hee-hee!" laughed Ernie. "Oops! Sorry, Bert."

"I was showing off on my roller skates at Miles's birthday party," said Big Bird, "and I fell flat on my feathers in front of everyone!"

"I got so sick to my stomach on the bus once that I had to ask the bus driver to stop!" said Ernie. "Everybody on the bus looked at me."

"I grabbed my mommy's hand in Nickles
Department Store once, only it wasn't my mommy!"
said Elmo. "It was some lady I had never seen before.
Boy, was I embarrassed."

"Yeah? You think those things are embarrassing?" asked Oscar. "I did something much worse than any of those little things."

"No!" they cried. "What did you do, Oscar?"

"I don't know what came over me," grumped Oscar. "I must have lost my senses."

"What did you *do*?" asked Big Bird.

"Well, Maria gave me this terrific present for my birthday. It was a crummy old bent fork."

"Yes, yes?" they asked eagerly.

"Well, I had to say thanks, of course. But then I kissed her!"

"No, Oscar!" Ernie said. "YOU kissed Maria?"

"It's true. I was so embarrassed!"

"That's all right, Oscar," said Bert. "Everybody gets embarrassed sometimes."

"Yeah, but you know what?" said Oscar. "Maria wasn't embarrassed at all!"